Coyote Goes Walking

Coyote Goes Walking

Retold and with pictures by

TOM POHRT

FARRAR   STRAUS   GIROUX   NEW   YORK

For Lynne

AUTHOR'S NOTE

The Coyote stories which appear in this book are based upon tales
collected in A. L. Kroeber's *Gros Ventre Myths and Tales*
and Robert H. Lowie's *The Assiniboine*.

Copyright © 1995 by Tom Pohrt
All rights reserved
Published simultaneously in Canada by HarperCollins*CanadaLtd*
Color separations by Hong Kong Scanner
Printed and bound in the United States of America
by Worzalla
Designed by Lilian Rosenstreich
First edition, 1995

Library of Congress Cataloging-in-Publication Data
Pohrt, Tom.
    Coyote goes walking / retold and illustrated by Tom Pohrt. — 1st ed.
        p.   cm.
    1. Indians of North America—Folklore.   2. Coyote (Legendary
character)—Legends.   3. Tales—North America.   [1. Coyote
(Legendary character)—Legends.   2. Indians of North America—
Folklore.].   I. Title.
E98.F6P64   1995   398.24'52974442—dc20   94-24096   CIP   AC

Contents

Introduction

Coyote, the animal, is playful and smart. He is a clever, resourceful hunter. Besides living in the wild, he has also adapted to suburban areas in many parts of Mexico, Canada, and much of the United States, including Alaska. In short, Coyote is a survivor.

The mythic figure of Coyote is also a survivor. In the following stories, which form part of an oral tradition stretching back into prehistory and continuing today among many Native American peoples, Coyote takes the prominent role of creator, messenger, and, above all, trickster. He is a mischievous character to be at once admired and feared, at times pitied, and often laughed at.

Coyote trickster stories reflect a great deal of humor and playfulness toward our own behavior and its consequences. In the same way that nature itself teaches us valuable lessons, Coyote, through his antics, teaches us the importance of listening, paying attention, and respecting all that surrounds us.

—TOM POHRT

Coyote Creates a New World

Sitting on top of a small mesa, Coyote saw that the people and animals around him had become too wild. So he decided to make a new world.

Coyote built a raft of buffalo chips, and when he was ready, he sang for the waters to come. For a long time it rained, until the entire earth was covered with water.

He was all alone, drifting on the water wherever the currents and winds took him. But after many days he grew tired of sitting on his raft.

Coyote had brought along his creation bundle. From this bundle he took the only other animals left: Loon, Heron, and Turtle. He sent Loon and Heron to the bottom of the water to bring up some mud, but they could not reach it. So Coyote breathed life into Turtle and asked him to try.

When Turtle came back, Coyote took the small bit of mud Turtle had brought him, and held it until it dried. Carefully opening and closing his paw, he sprinkled the dried mud back into the water, creating land where it dropped.

From the newly made earth Coyote scooped out some clay and began to mold it into birds, insects, fish—all the animals, female and male. Then he molded the two-legged beings.

Coyote took great delight in naming them, and repeating their names again and again in the many languages of the creatures he'd created. Coyote blew life into them, and they came alive. The world was filled with a wonderful noise!

Coyote went walking.

Coyote and Mice

One day, while Coyote was walking around, he heard singing.

"There is a Sun dance going on around here somewhere," he said.

Coyote wanted to discover where the singing was coming from. First he ran one way, listening; then he ran the other way. But he always came back to the same place.

When Coyote sat down on an elk skull to try to figure out why he couldn't find the music, he heard the noise of the dance clearly.

"This must be the place I was looking for all along," he said, laughing.

He looked into the eye socket of the elk skull and saw some mice holding a Sun dance.

"I WOULD LIKE TO COME IN!" Coyote shouted over the singing.

"YOU CAN'T COME IN!" the mice shouted back. They knew Coyote.

Coyote then spoke to the eye socket. "Become larger," he said, and it did. As often as he told it to grow larger, it did. Finally he succeeded in making the eye socket big enough to get his head through.

Most of the mice ran out, except a few who stayed behind to say, "You always cause trouble, Coyote!"

Coyote tried to take the skull off, but it was stuck. He started to cry because he did not know what to do. He could not even see! Coyote got up and wandered off as the last of the mice jumped from the skull. He hit something with his foot and said, "Who are you?"

"I am a cherry tree," it said.

"I must be near the river," said Coyote.

He continued to feel about with his feet. He stubbed his foot on something else. "Ow! Who are you?"

"I am a cottonwood tree," it said.

"I must be getting closer to the river," Coyote said and went on. Again he struck his foot on something. His foot was really hurting now.

"Well, who are you?" Coyote said.

"I am a willow tree," it said.

"I must be right next to the river," Coyote said. "I can even hear it!" And just then he fell down the riverbank and broke the skull in two against some rocks. Coyote looked around, dazed, and felt the top of his head, which was quite bald, for the mice who had stayed behind for a moment had chewed up a patch of his hair. Coyote was angry and called the mice many bad names.

Coyote and Woodpecker

Coyote was out walking in the woods. He noticed that Woodpecker was sitting on a limb in front of the tree lodge where he lived with his wife and children.

"Ha! Coyote!" shouted Woodpecker. "I saw you coming. My wife is heating water. You must stay and eat with us. I am just going to get some food."

Coyote watched Woodpecker fly to an old pine tree and begin to peck at the bark with his beak. Up the tree Woodpecker went, pecking hard and fast. He made a lot of noise! Coyote had never seen anyone collect food like this before.

At last Woodpecker had gathered a big supply of worms, which he brought home to cook. Coyote climbed up into Woodpecker's lodge and sat down. It was crowded, but Coyote liked the food. When Coyote was ready to leave, he thanked Woodpecker and his family and invited them to come for a meal at his lodge in a couple of days.

After two days passed, Woodpecker said to his wife, "It's time to go visit Coyote and see what he has fixed for us to eat."

When Woodpecker and his family arrived at Coyote's camp, they found him high up in a tree.

"Ha! Woodpecker!" Coyote said. "I'll be with you in a moment. The water is boiling, and I am just getting some food here!"

Coyote had carved a beak out of wood—it looked something like Woodpecker's beak—and it was tied over his snout.

Coyote began to peck at the tree. It hurt his nose and mouth each time he pecked. But Coyote was not making a good hole in the tree to get at the worms, so he pecked harder. And the harder he pecked, the more dizzy he became with pain. His eyes began to water. Finally, with one giant peck, Coyote knocked himself out and fell to the ground. Woodpecker and his family rushed over to help him.

"Ha! My friend," said Woodpecker, "this is not your way to get food!"

Woodpecker flew to the pine tree and collected a big supply of worms. Woodpecker and his family cooked them at Coyote's lodge. The meal was delicious, and everyone, including Coyote, had a good laugh at his misfortune. But Coyote was still a little dizzy.

Coyote and the Buffalo Bull

Coyote was taking a walk along the riverbank when he spied a buffalo bull skull on top of a pile of rocks. Coyote went over and knocked the skull off the rocks, into the river.

"I'm not afraid of that old buffalo bull now," Coyote said, laughing.

Later that same day, Coyote was walking by the same spot, and there was the buffalo bull's skull BACK on the pile of rocks. Hmmmm, this is odd, he thought. Once again Coyote knocked the skull to the ground. Then he took a big, flat rock and smashed the skull, kicking the pieces into the river. "That's that!" said Coyote.

But just as he started to walk away, he heard a snorting and the sound of a buffalo stomping the ground. When

Coyote turned, he stood facing the old buffalo bull, large
as life—bigger, in fact—and angry! The old buffalo charged
at Coyote, who ran off with a yelp.

Coyote leaped into a crack in a rock barely large enough
for him to fit in. The buffalo bull butted the rock with his
head, and it broke into a thousand pieces.

Coyote was stunned but managed to jump into a large
hollow tree stump. The old buffalo hooked the tree with
his horns and flung it up over his head, sending Coyote

sailing through the air into a small lake. Then the buffalo
bull began to lap up all the water until Coyote was left
crawling along the muddy lake bottom.

"Spare me," said Coyote. "I've had enough!"

"Coyote, you kicked my skull into the river both times you walked by. This place is sacred ground for many of us, and you show great disrespect by what you did. Now you must hurry and make me tobacco from willow tree bark."

Coyote was so scared he was shaking, but he did as he was told, and soon presented the tobacco to the old buffalo bull. The old buffalo placed the tobacco in a pipe and lit it by holding it up toward the sun. He sat and smoked. The colors and light of the setting sun began to flicker through the old bull's hide as he slowly disappeared before Coyote's eyes.

Down by the riverbank, a clean white skull appeared atop a pile of rocks.

Coyote turned and walked away.